DISCARD

Cultural Traditions in Cuba

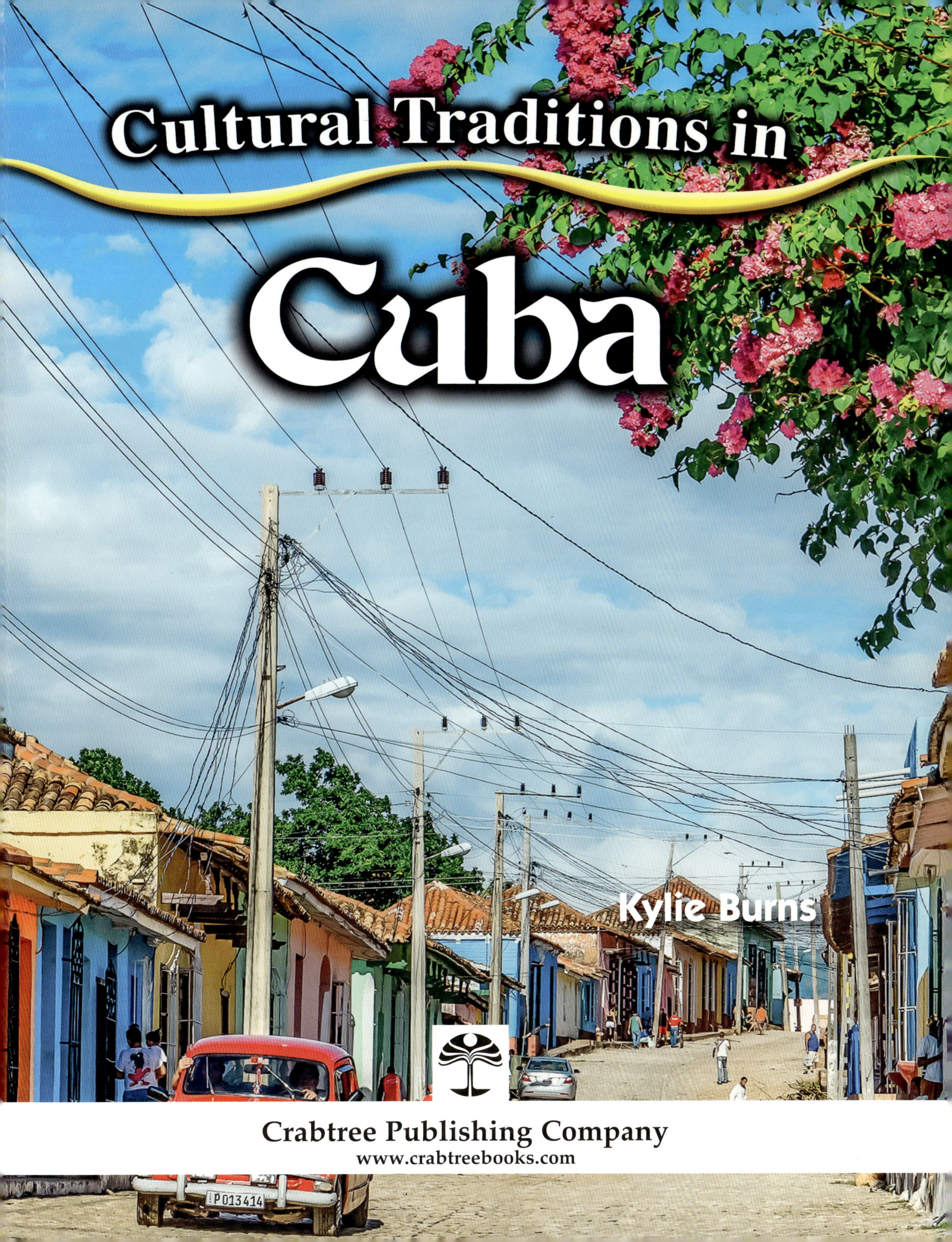

Kylie Burns

Crabtree Publishing Company
www.crabtreebooks.com

Crabtree Publishing Company
www.crabtreebooks.com

Author: Kylie Burns

Publishing plan research and development:
Reagan Miller

Editorial director: Kathy Middleton

Editor: Janine Deschenes

Proofreader: Wendy Scavuzzo

Photo research: Abigail Smith

Designer: Abigail Smith

Production coordinator and prepress technician:
Abigail Smith

Print coordinator: Margaret Amy Salter

Cover: The Cathedral of Nuestra Senora de la Asunción in Santiago de Cuba (top, background); Cuba's national bird, the trogon (middle); white ginger lily flower (middle left); rumba dancer (bottom right); Cuban jazz trumpeter (bottom left)

Title page: A colorful street in the town of Trinidad.

Photographs:
Alamy: Newzulu, p18; Hemis, p22; Hemis, p26; age fotostock, p27 (bottom)
Getty Images: ADALBERTO ROQUE, p25; YAMIL LAGE, p25; Roberto Machado Noa, p30 (left); David Silverman, p31 (top)
iStock: GemaBlanton, p7 (left); bst2012, p7 (right); Image Source, p9; Nikada, p23 (top); ArtMarie, p23 (botom)
Shutterstock: © Kamira, Cover (bottom left); © Kobby Dagan, Cover (right); © Anna Jedynak, title page, p17; © Hang Dinh, p5 (botom); © akturer, p5 (right); © javier gonzalez leyva, p8; © Maurizio De Mattei, p10; © T photography, p11; © Emily Marie Wilson, p11 (inset); © marcin jucha, p13 (bottom); © Rob Crandall, p13 (inset); © Gil.K, p14; © Maros Markovic, p19; © Oleg Golovnev, p19 (inset); © Tupungato, p21 (bottom)
Wikimedia Commons: Creative Commons, p15 (inset); Public Domain, p27 (inset)

All other images by Shutterstock

Library and Archives Canada Cataloguing in Publication

Burns, Kylie, author
    Cultural traditions in Cuba / Kylie Burns.

(Cultural traditions in my world)
Includes index.
Issued in print and electronic formats.
ISBN 978-0-7787-8094-6 (hardcover).--
ISBN 978-0-7787-8102-8 (softcover).--
ISBN 978-1-4271-1949-0 (HTML)

    1. Holidays--Cuba--Juvenile literature. 2. Festivals--Cuba--Juvenile literature. 3. Cuba--Social life and customs--Juvenile literature. I. Title. II. Series: Cultural traditions in my world

GT4825.A2B87 2017   j394.2697291   C2017-903509-6
    C2017-903510-X

Library of Congress Cataloging-in-Publication Data

Names: Burns, Kylie, author.
Title: Cultural traditions in Cuba / Kylie Burns.
Description: New York : Crabtree Publishing Company, 2017. |
Series: Cultural traditions in my world | Includes index. | Audience: Age 5-8. | Audience: Grade K to grade 3.
Identifiers: LCCN 2017024401 (print) | LCCN 2017025422 (ebook) |
  ISBN 9781427119490 (Electronic HTML) |
  ISBN 9780778780946 (reinforced library binding) |
  ISBN 9780778781028 (pbk.)
Subjects: LCSH: Festivals--Cuba--Juvenile literature. | Cuba--Social life and customs--Juvenile literature.
Classification: LCC GT4825.A2 (ebook) | LCC GT4825.A2 B87 2017 (print) | DDC 394.2697291--dc23
LC record available at https://lccn.loc.gov/2017024401

Crabtree Publishing Company
www.crabtreebooks.com   1-800-387-7650

Printed in Canada/082017/EF20170629

Copyright © **2018 CRABTREE PUBLISHING COMPANY**. All rights reserved. No part of this publication may be reproduced, stored in a retrieval system or be transmitted in any form or by any means, electronic, mechanical, photocopying, recording, or otherwise, without the prior written permission of Crabtree Publishing Company. In Canada: We acknowledge the financial support of the Government of Canada through the Canada Book Fund for our publishing activities.

Published in Canada
Crabtree Publishing
616 Welland Ave.
St. Catharines, ON
L2M 5V6

Published in the United States
Crabtree Publishing
PMB 59051
350 Fifth Avenue, 59th Floor
New York, New York 10118

Published in the United Kingdom
Crabtree Publishing
Maritime House
Basin Road North, Hove
BN41 1WR

Published in Australia
Crabtree Publishing
3 Charles Street
Coburg North
VIC 3058

Contents

Welcome to Cuba 4
Birthdays and Quinceañara 6
Weddings 8
Celebrating the Arts 10
New Year and Liberation Day 12
José Martí's Birthday Memorial 14
Good Friday and Easter.......... 16
May Day 18
Independence Day 20
Children's Day 22
National Revolution Day 24
Carnival of Santiago de Cuba 26
Anniversary of the Beginning of the
    Wars of Independence........ 28
Christmas and Epiphany 30
Glossary and Index............ 32

Welcome to Cuba

The **Republic** of Cuba is a group of tropical islands. It includes the largest island in the Caribbean. Cuba is surrounded by three large bodies of water: the Caribbean Sea, the Atlantic Ocean, and the Gulf of Mexico. More than 11 million people call Cuba home. The country's official language is Spanish. There are many special cultural traditions, or customs, in Cuba.

Cubans sometimes call their country El Cocodrilo which is Spanish for "crocodile," because the island appears to have the shape of a crocodile.

Cuba's traditions come from its many different cultures, such as Spanish, African, French, South American, and Taíno. The Taíno are **Indigenous** people native to Cuba. Most holidays focus on special events in Cuba's history, or **religious** celebrations. Celebrations often include traditional music and dances.

Did You Know?
Music and dance are an important part of Cuban culture. The dancers in this picture are performing a dance called the Salsa.

Cuba's colorful, busy capital city is called Havana.

Birthdays and Quinceañera

Birthdays are important family celebrations in Cuba. It is a custom for families, friends, and neighbors to gather for a child's birthday party. Singing, dancing, and feasting on birthday cake are traditional birthday activities. Many parents hire clowns or magicians to provide fun and games for the children. Piñatas, balloons, and music are important, too.

Did You Know?
Instead of hitting the piñata, people in Cuba pull on ribbons at the bottom to release the treats, such as candies, pencils, or small toys.

When Cuban girls turn 15, they have a party called a quinceañera. This event traditionally celebrates a girl's change from childhood to adulthood. Hundreds of years ago, fifteen was the age when most women married. Today, parents throw a fancy party for their daughter, gathering family and friends together.

Girls wear ball gowns on their quinceañera, and often have a special photoshoot.

It is traditional for girls to perform a special father-daughter dance.

Weddings

Before a Cuban wedding ceremony, family and friends line the street and wish the bride and groom happiness for the future. The parents of the bride usually pay for the wedding, which includes a fiesta, or party. After the fiesta, the bride and groom give each guest a handmade gift or a Cuban cigar to thank them for celebrating their wedding day.

On their wedding day, a bride and groom in Cuba travel around town in a decorated convertible car.

Cuban weddings include some interesting traditions. Guests take part in a money dance, where they dance with the bride and pin money on her dress. A Cuban wedding cake, shown below, is baked with several ribbons inside. The ends of the ribbons hang outside the cake. One has a ring tied to it inside the cake. Each unmarried girl at a wedding pulls a ribbon from the cake. Tradition says that the girl who pulls the ribbon with the ring will be the next to get married.

Celebrating the Arts

Dance, theater, and film are important in Cuba. The country has a large arts community. Music is a big part of Cuban life. Son Cubano, or Son, is a popular type of music in Cuba. It is used as the music of many Cuban dances. Several of these famous dances include the Mambo, Rumba, Cha Cha Cha, and the Pachanga.

Did You Know?
Cuban music blends African and Spanish **rhythms**, sounds, and instruments. Some of those instruments include the *tres*, or Cuban guitar, and the voices of the singers, called *sonera*.

The award-winning Ballet Nacional de Cuba, or Cuban National Ballet, was officially started in 1960. Boys and girls are both given an opportunity to attend ballet school, and the Cuban government pays for all of their training—which takes 8 years to complete. Many dancers go on international tours with the Ballet, giving them the chance to see the world.

The Great Theater of Havana, located in Cuba's capital city, is home to the Ballet Nacional de Cuba. Havana hosts an international ballet festival every two years.

New Year and Liberation Day

Cubans celebrate the end of the year on December 31. Together with family and friends, they practice many traditions on this day. Some Cubans eat 12 grapes at midnight—one for every month of the year. Others place money in their own mailboxes as a symbol of their hope to make more money in the coming year. At midnight, people dance in the streets while fireworks explode in the sky.

Black beans with rice is a popular food in Cuba. On New Year's Eve, it is served with grilled meats such as chicken, turkey, or a whole roasted pig.

In Cuba, January 1 is Liberation Day. Liberation means freedom. It is a national holiday because it is the anniversary of the Triumph of the **Revolution**—an important event in Cuba's history. On this day, Cubans celebrate the end of one kind of government, and the beginning of a new government with a new leader. There is music and dancing, outdoor discos, and a parade.

Did You Know?
On January 1, 1959, Fidel Castro (right) became the leader of the Republic of Cuba. He was leader until 2008, a total of 49 years.

Good Friday and Easter

Good Friday and Easter are **Christian** holidays that celebrate the death and **resurrection** of Jesus Christ. Banks and schools are closed for the day. On Easter, Cuban **Catholics** celebrate by attending mass at a local church, followed by a feast prepared by family and friends who gather together for the meal.

Cubans eat *bacalao*, or codfish, on Good Friday. It is custom to avoid eating flesh other than fish on this day.

At 3 p.m. on Good Friday, bells ring at all of Havana's churches. They remind Catholics to remember the death of Jesus Christ on a cross.

Another traditional Easter celebration in Cuba takes place every March in the town of Trinidad. Catholics participate in walking a long route through the town to remember the walk that Jesus Christ took on the way to his death on a cross. This is known as the Way of the Cross.

During the Way of The Cross, this quiet street is lined with hundreds of people.

Did You Know? Many Cubans create crosses out of palm leaves to carry or hang in their homes at Easter.

May Day

In Cuba, May Day is a national holiday that is celebrated on May 1. In many other countries, it is known as Labor Day. Large parades are held all over Cuba on May Day. The largest is in Havana, shown below.

Did You Know?
May Day celebrations begin with singing the Cuban National Anthem, and end with chants, cheers, and festivities with family and friends.

During May Day parades, Cubans carry signs and posters with messages that support workers. In Havana, more than one million people gather in Revolution Square. Cultural performances, entertainment, and speeches by government leaders are all part of Havana's May Day celebration.

Agriculture, or farming, is one of the largest **industries** in Cuba. Farm workers in Cuba help grow important products such as sugar, tobacco, and coffee.

Independence Day

On May 20, Cuba celebrates gaining independence from Spain following the War of Independence. Throughout the 1800s, Cubans fought to break away from Spain's rule over their country. They were finally successful in 1898, when Cuba defeated Spain with the help of the United States.

The white stripes represent peace.

The three sides of the red triangle shape represent equality, liberty, and brotherly love.

The three blue stripes represent Cuba's three **regions**—central, east, and west.

The white star represents freedom or independence.

Did You Know?
The Cuban flag was created by a general in the Spanish Army who supported Cuban independence. The flag's colors and symbols have different meanings.

Red represents blood shed during the War of Independence.

Cuba's became officially independent on May 20, 1902. Many Cubans honor Independence Day by having a traditional meal with family. Traditional Cuban meals might include rice and beans, or a stew made with beef, tomato, and vegetables. Roast pig is also a traditional Cuban dish.

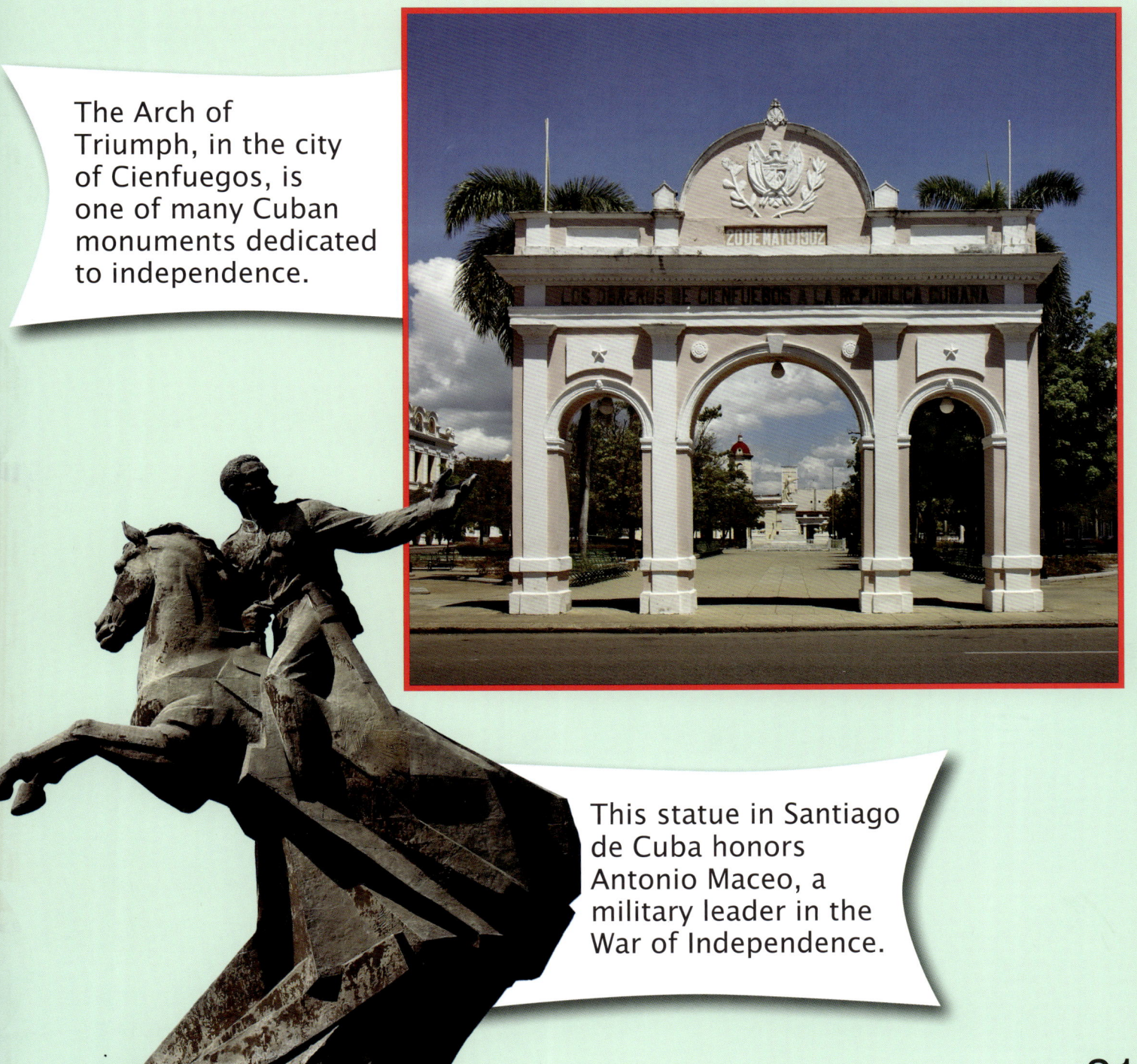

The Arch of Triumph, in the city of Cienfuegos, is one of many Cuban monuments dedicated to independence.

This statue in Santiago de Cuba honors Antonio Maceo, a military leader in the War of Independence.

Children's Day

Children in Cuba are respected as the future of the country. Cuba celebrates Children's Day, called Día del Niño, on June 1. Many festive activities are organized, and children are often given sweets or toys from their parents. They may visit an amusement park, or the zoo with their families. There are outdoor concerts, plays, and sports games to enjoy as well. Movie theaters show children's movies. It is a day-long party all over the country.

These children are enjoying a Children's Day parade in the city of Santiago de Cuba.

Many Cuban children are involved in sports and other activities outside of school, including baseball, soccer, boxing, volleyball, and dance. Most children grow up without a television or computer, so they are often found playing games outside in the streets.

Did You Know?
Baseball is the most popular sport in Cuba.

All Cuban students wear uniforms to school.

National Revolution Day

Revolution Day, on July 26, is a day of national pride for Cubans. After Cuba became independent, it was ruled by many different leaders who treated the Cuban people unfairly. On July 26, 1953, a group of **rebels**, led by Fidel Castro, led an attack that began the Cuban revolution. They wanted to remove the country's leader, President Batista. The rebels did not win this battle, but were finally successful in 1959. Fidel Castro became the new leader of Cuba.

On Revolution Day in 2006, Fidel Castro gives a speech to the Cuban people.

Cubans also celebrate the day before Revolution Day (July 25), and the day after (July 27). For three days, there are speeches, parades, and parties. A red-and-black flag with the date of the Revolution's beginning is the symbol of Revolution Day, and it can be seen waving proudly during Revolution Day celebrations.

Did You Know?
National Revolution Day is the largest of all of Cuba's holidays.

26 JULIO

On Revolution Day, many Cubans dress in traditional clothing, and take part in parades and dances.

Carnival of Santiago de Cuba

Cuba's largest carnival takes place in Santiago de Cuba. Each year from July 18 to 27, people come from all over Cuba and the world to attend the Carnival of Santiago de Cuba. Celebrations include parties in the streets, parades with floats, and people wearing colorful costumes.

Did You Know?
The carnival celebrates the history of many groups in Cuba. It also honors the Revolution.

The Carnival's history goes back even farther than Cuba's Revolution. It began as a Christian festival, and also comes from traditional summer festivals, called *mamarrachos*. These were celebrations that included elements of African, Spanish, French, and Indigenous cultures. Conga music is a rhythmic blend of sounds and beats from these cultures that can be heard throughout the entire festival.

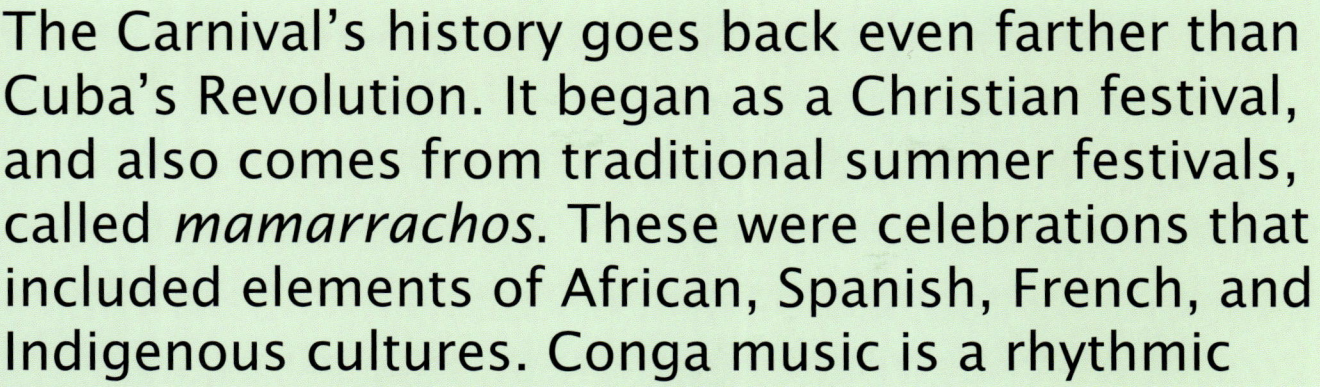

Street performers play Conga music during one of the many parades of the Santiago Festival.

Did You Know?
People join the parades dressed in elaborate costumes, including huge heads made from paper, glue, and paint.

Anniversary of the Beginning of the Wars of Independence

There were three wars between Cuba and Spain that led to Cuba's independence. The first war began on October 10, 1868. That day, a wealthy landowner, Carlos Manuel de Céspedes, decided to free 30 men who were working as his **slaves**. Those slaves and many other Cubans joined together to fight for independence from Spain. Though they did not win, this date is the official beginning of the wars of independence in Cuba. Today, October 10 is a national holiday in Cuba. Many Cubans have a day off work or school, and spend the day with friends and family.

Cubans celebrate by gathering at the park in Plaza de Armas, Havana, where the monument of Carlos Manuel de Céspedes stands. They lay flower wreaths there.

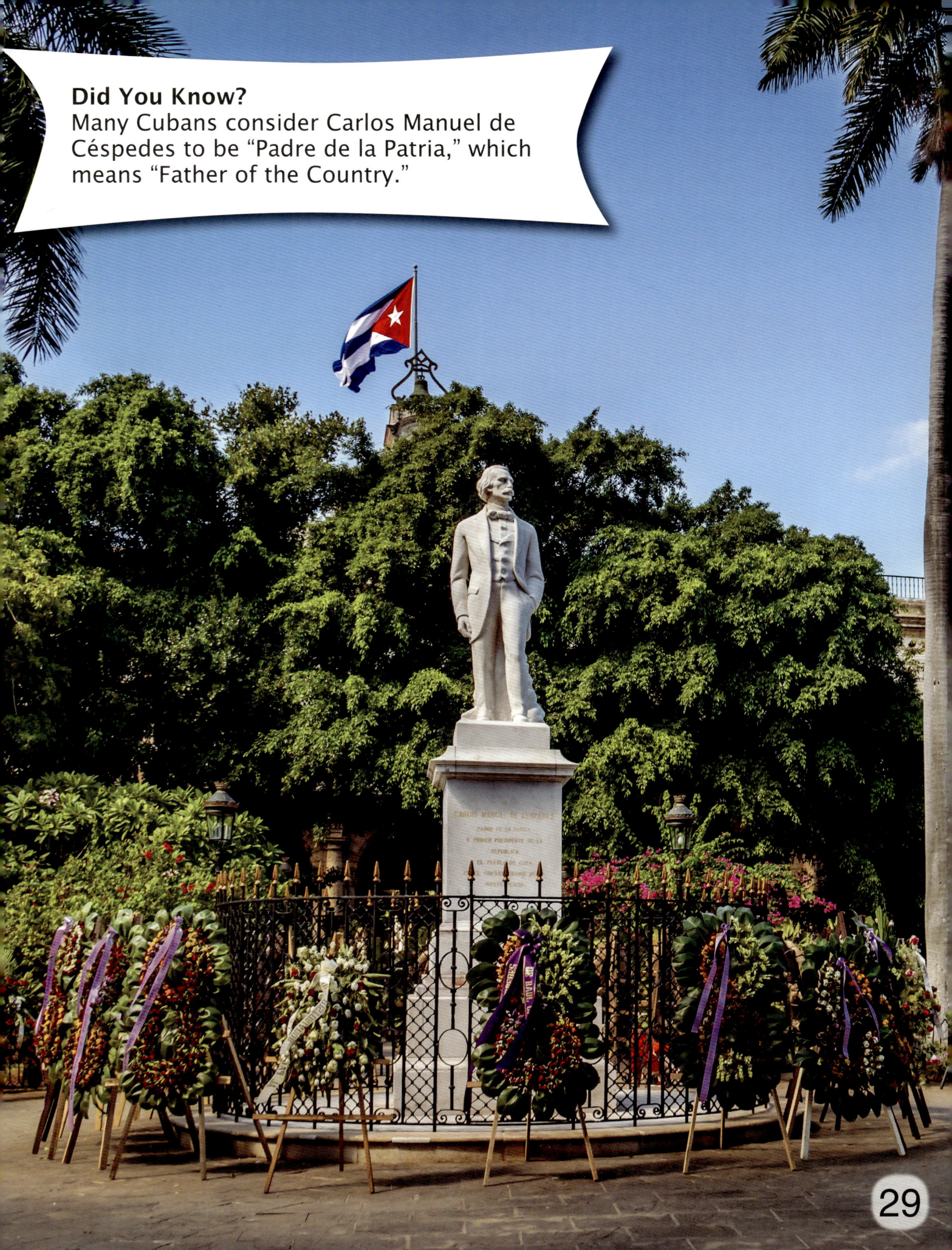

Did You Know?
Many Cubans consider Carlos Manuel de Céspedes to be "Padre de la Patria," which means "Father of the Country."

Christmas and Epiphany

On December 24, Noche Buena (Christmas Eve) is celebrated in Cuba. It is a Christian celebration of the birth of Jesus Christ. Families get together for a huge dinner which often includes roast pork, rice and black beans, boiled **cassava** in garlic sauce, and fried plantains. After dinner, many Cubans attend a midnight church service. The following day is Christmas Day, a national holiday.

Fried plantains are a popular snack and side dish in many Caribbean and South American countries.

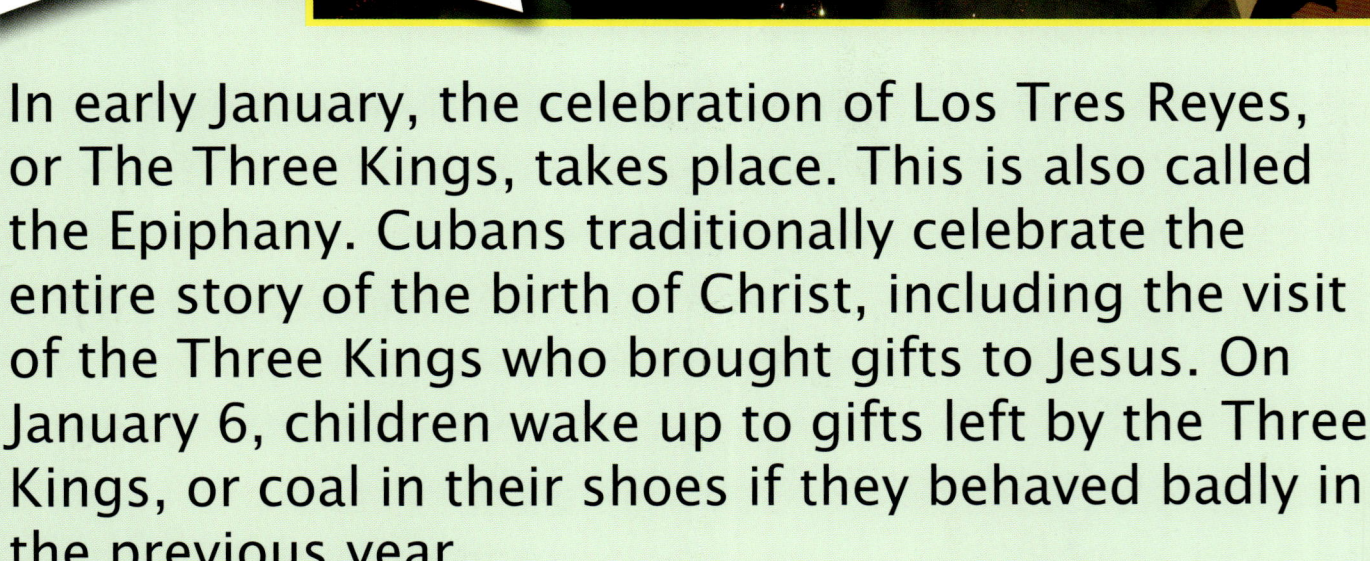

Did You Know?
Each year, the city of Remedios hosts Las Parrandas—a Christmas festival that lasts up to 10 days in December. Two teams, called the roosters and the hawks, compete to create the best light display in a fireworks competition.

In early January, the celebration of Los Tres Reyes, or The Three Kings, takes place. This is also called the Epiphany. Cubans traditionally celebrate the entire story of the birth of Christ, including the visit of the Three Kings who brought gifts to Jesus. On January 6, children wake up to gifts left by the Three Kings, or coal in their shoes if they behaved badly in the previous year.

The **nativity scene** is an important part of the Cuban Christmas tradition. Each day before January 6, children move the Three Kings closer to the baby Jesus. The evening of January 5, the children leave hay and water out for the camels that carry the Three Kings to deliver gifts at all the children's homes.

Glossary

cassava The starchy root of a tree used for food

Catholics A branch of Christianity, led by the Pope

Christian Someone who follows the teachings of Jesus Christ, whom they believe to be the Son of God

independent Free to rule itself

Indigenous Living, growing, or occuring naturally in a place

industries Workers and companies that produce a particular type of product, such as food

nativity scene A scene showing the Baby Jesus with his mother Mary, father Joseph, and Three Kings

rebels People who form a group that goes against a government or ruler

regions An area or part of a place

religious Having faith or following a faith, or religion

republic A country or state in which citizens vote for their leaders

resurrection To come back from the dead

revolution The overthrow of one government or leader for another

rhythmic A steady, repeated beat

slaves People who were forced to work for an owner without pay

Index

Castro, Fidel 13, 24
Céspedes, Carlos Manuel de 28, 29
costumes 25, 26, 27
dance 5, 6, 7, 9, 10, 11, 12, 13, 23, 25
farming 19
fireworks 12, 31
flags 14, 20, 25
foods 12, 16, 21, 30
Havana 5, 11, 15, 16, 18, 19, 28
Martí, José 14, 15
monuments 15, 21, 28
music 5, 6, 10, 13, 27
national holidays 13, 16, 18, 20, 24, 28, 30
nativity scene 31
parades 13, 14, 18, 19, 22, 24, 25, 26, 27
piñatas 6
Revolution 13, 14, 15, 19, 24, 25, 26, 27
Santiago de Cuba 21, 22, 26, 27
sports 22, 23
Taíno people 4, 5